Little Princesses

The Silk Princess

3

www.**kids**at**random**house.co.uk/littleprincesses

THE *Little Princesses* SERIES

The Whispering Princess

The Fairytale Princess

The Peach Blossom Princess

The Rain Princess

The Snowflake Princess

The Dream-catcher Princess

The Desert Princess

The Lullaby Princess

The Silk Princess

The Cloud Princess

The Sea Princess

The Golden Princess

Little Princesses
The Silk Princess

By Katie Chase

Illustrated by Leighton Noyes

Red Fox

Special thanks to Narinder Dhami

THE SILK PRINCESS
A RED FOX BOOK 9780099488385

First published in Great Britain by Red Fox,
an imprint of Random House Children's Books

This edition published 2007

3 5 7 9 10 8 6 4 2

Series created by Working Partners Ltd
Copyright © Working Partners Ltd, 2007
Illustrations copyright © Leighton Noyes, 2007
Cover illustration by Nila Aye

Set in 15/21pt Bembo Schoolbook

Red Fox Books are published by Random House Children's Books,
61–63 Uxbridge Road, London W5 5SA,
a division of The Random House Group Ltd

Addresses for Random House Group Ltd companies outside the UK
can be found at: www.randomhouse.co.uk

THE RANDOM HOUSE GROUP Limited Reg. No. 954009
www.kidsatrandomhouse.co.uk

The Random House Group Limited makes every effort to ensure that the
papers used in its books are made from trees that have been legally
sourced from well-managed and credibly certified forests. Our paper
procurement policy can be found at: www.randomhouse.co.uk/paper.htm.

Mixed Sources
Product group from well-managed
forests and other controlled sources
www.fsc.org Cert no. TT-COC-2139
© 1996 Forest Stewardship Council
FSC

A CIP catalogue record for this book is available from the British Library.

Printed and bound in Great Britain by
Cox & Wyman Ltd, Reading, Berkshire

For Marilyn Lazarou.
Simply the Best. – *M.J.L.*

For Jayne-Ann,
with love – *L.N.*

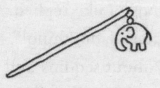

Chapter One

"Come on, Rosie!" called Luke excitedly, as he charged through the huge wooden door into the castle. "I want *my* picture frame to be the best one in the whole class!"

Rosie grinned as she followed her younger brother inside. Luke's teacher had asked the class to find things at home that they could use to decorate a picture frame, and Luke was keen to get started.

"I bet we can find lots of stuff around the castle," Rosie said. "I'm sure Great-aunt Rosamund will have some lovely bits and pieces you can use."

"My teacher said we should look out for

all sorts of things," Luke replied. "Buttons, foil, bits of material, anything!"

"And what about sequins and sparkly glitter?" Rosie suggested.

"Great! I'll look upstairs first," Luke said eagerly, and he shot off up the wide oak staircase. Rosie followed him, just in time to see their dad come out of the main bedroom.

"Luke, watch out!" yelled Rosie. But she was too late. Luke bumped straight into Mr Campbell, who looked very surprised.

"What's all this?" he laughed, raising his eyebrows. "I didn't know a tornado had just

hit the Scottish Highlands! Slow down,
Luke."

"Sorry, Dad." Luke said, hopping
impatiently from one foot to the other.
"I have to find stuff for my art lesson!"

"OK, just be careful," Mr Campbell
warned. "Remember that a lot of Great-aunt
Rosamund's things are very valuable."

Luke nodded.

"We could start in the sewing room,"
Rosie called up the stairs. "There are lots of
cool things in there." But her brother had
already disappeared along the landing.

Smiling to herself, Rosie carried on up the
stairs and wandered down the corridor
towards her great-aunt's sewing room. Great-
aunt Rosamund loved travelling, and her
sewing room was full of fabrics, beads and
bric-a-brac from all over the world.

Now she was away again on another long

trip. This time she had asked Rosie
and her family to move in and look
after her beautiful Scottish castle
while she was away. Rosie could
hardly believe how lucky she was.

Rosie gazed around the room.
The walls were lined with shelves,
which were crammed with silks,
satins and velvets in every colour
of the rainbow. There were baskets
filled with spools of coloured thread,
as well as sequins, buttons and
tapestry wools. A large, old-
fashioned sewing machine stood in
one corner and a tailor's dummy
in another, draped with rose-red silk.

Rosie went over to look at a
basket of buttons. As she did so, a
photograph next to the sewing
machine caught her eye. It showed

Great-aunt Rosamund
sitting on an elephant!
Rosie grinned. Her great-
aunt was wearing a pink
and gold sari and carrying
a fringed parasol.

This photo must have been taken in India,
Rosie thought, remembering that her great-
aunt had told her stories about her trip to
India. She picked up the photo for a closer
look, and her gaze fell on the frame
surrounding the picture. It was made out of
silk and was beautifully embroidered with
threads of many different colours. In one
corner of the frame was a tiny woven picture
of a young girl, who was also sitting on an
elephant. She had long, black hair, pinned
up with a pretty hairpin, which had a tiny
sparkling elephant dangling from it.

Rosie gasped. "It's another little princess!"

she said to herself. "I'm sure of it!"

Before going on her travels, Great-aunt
Rosamund had left behind a secret letter for
Rosie, telling her to look out for
little princesses hidden in pictures all over the
castle. Whenever Rosie found one of the
princesses, she always ended up having
a wonderful adventure!

Shaking with excitement,
Rosie sank into a low
curtsey, just as her
great-aunt had
insructed.

"Hello!" she
whispered.

Immediately, a warm breeze
swept towards Rosie from the picture frame.
As it lifted her gently off her feet, Rosie
closed her eyes. She could smell the
strong scent of jasmine and exotic spices. The

breeze grew stronger, and Rosie knew
that she was being whirled away to a
far-off land.

A second or two later the breeze died
away. Rosie could feel the sun beating
down on her and hear noise all around.
Quickly she opened her eyes.

She was standing in the middle of a busy,
bustling market. There was a stall nearby,
piled high with colourful fruit and vegetables,
many of which Rosie didn't recognize. Large
silver dishes of spices in red, gold, orange
and green were also for sale, along with silver
and gold jewellery set with sparkling gems,
and heavily-embroidered bedspreads and
tablecloths decorated with tiny mirrors.

People hurried through the market,
bargaining with the stallholders. The men
wore loose trousers and shirts, and some wore
turbans, while the women were dressed in saris.

"I must be in India!" Rosie told herself. She glanced down and was delighted to see that she too wore a sari. It was made of lilac chiffon, shot through with dazzling silver threads, and she had matching silver sandals on her feet.

Rosie wondered where the little princess could be. She stared round at the stalls, but the girl from the picture frame was nowhere to be seen.

I'd better go and find her, Rosie thought. So she set off, weaving her way through the crowds of people.

After a few minutes, Rosie found herself on the edge of the market. She was in a street of small wooden shops, lined with trees. It was quieter here, though monkeys chattered and swung through the branches overhead. Rosie frowned; she couldn't see anyone else around. Where *could* the little princess be?

At that moment a young girl with long black hair came out of one of the shops. She was carrying an apricot-coloured sari in her arms. Rosie's heart began to beat faster, because the girl looked just like the little princess!

Rosie watched the girl throw the sari into a large wooden tub of water, which stood outside the shop front. There were brown onionskins floating in the tub, and the water was a sludgy brown colour.

The girl took a stick and began stirring the sari energetically in the water. As she did so, the beautiful apricot colour started to disappear, and the material turned the same dull brown colour as the water.

Rosie was puzzled. Why would anyone want to make a beautiful apricot sari that horrible shade of brown? As she wondered about this, she spotted a washing-line strung between two nearby trees. It was hung with other brown saris, which had obviously just been dyed too.

The other girl bent lower over the tub of water, and her hair swung forward. As it did so, Rosie could see a tiny elephant dangling from a hairpin.

Now she was sure that this really *was* the little princess, Rosie hurried forwards. "Hello!" she called, "I'm so glad I've found you. I'm Rosie, and you must be the little princess!"

The girl stopped stirring the water and looked up at Rosie with a puzzled smile. "What do you mean?" she asked. "*I'm* not a princess!"

Chapter Two

Rosie's mouth dropped open. She was so
shocked, she couldn't speak.

"But you *must* be!" Rosie spluttered.

The girl shook her head, frowning. "Oh,
but I'm not!" she said firmly. "I don't own
anything valuable, and I don't live in a
palace. I can't be a princess."

"Are you sure?" Rosie asked desperately.

The girl nodded. "A princess would have
jewels and gold and servants. All I have in the
world are the two things my mother left me
when she died. This hairpin is one of them,"
she added, pointing to her hair.

"Oh, I *am* sorry to hear about your

 13 ★

mother!" Rosie said. "You and your father must miss her very much."

The girl bit her lip sadly. "My father has passed away too," she said quietly. "He and my mother both died when I was very young. . ."

"But you're not all alone?" asked Rosie anxiously.

"No, my Uncle Bansi looks after me," the girl replied, brightening. "He's a silk trader and tailor, just like my father was. He's very kind to me."

Rosie smiled to hear that, but she was very confused. She couldn't believe this girl *wasn't* a little princess. The magic *always* brought her to a princess, surely it couldn't have made a mistake?

Suddenly a thought struck her. "Are you in disguise?" she asked in a whisper. "You can tell me if you are. I can keep a secret, I promise."

The girl burst out laughing. "I'm not in
disguise!" she giggled. "My name is Suvita,
and I help my uncle in his silk shop." She
pointed at the wooden shop front behind
them. "He's away at the moment, selling his
silks, but if you need anything, maybe I can
help?"

Rosie frowned thoughtfully. "Is there a
royal palace nearby?" she asked, thinking
that if Suvita wasn't the girl she was looking
for, then she should probably go and try to
find the *real* little princess.

Suvita nodded, staring curiously at Rosie. "It's not far from here, but why do you want to know?" she asked.

"I'm looking for a princess," Rosie explained. "You see, I came here by magic – my Great-aunt Rosamund told me how—"

"Rosamund?" Suvita interrupted, frowning. "I know that name. I think my mother might have mentioned it to me, many years ago – what a strange coincidence!"

Rosie felt even more confused. "That's very odd," she agreed, thinking hard. It was clear that Suvita was the girl on the photo frame and, like the other princesses Rosie had met, she recognized Rosamund's name – and yet she *wasn't* a princess!

"If you want to go to the palace, I can draw you a map," Suvita was saying. "But I must finish dyeing the silks first." She began pulling the sari, now a dirty brown colour, out of the water. "You do realize that you won't find the missing princess at the palace, though, don't you?"

"The princess is missing?" Rosie cried, her heart skipping a beat. Maybe *that* was why she had been whisked to India: to *find* the little princess!

Suvita nodded. "It's because of the missing princess that I'm dyeing all these beautiful silks," she sighed. She began hanging the sari on the washing-line, and Rosie hurried to help her.

"What happened?" Rosie asked eagerly.

Suvita smiled. "You must have come from

far, far away if you've never heard of the
missing princess of Ranavhata!" she told
Rosie. "She's very famous. I'll tell you the
whole story."

Chapter Three

"Some time before I was born," Suvita began, "there was a beautiful princess who was the apple of her father's eye. The Maharajah of Ranavhata was so proud of her that he wanted her to marry a prince from a neighbouring kingdom; no one else was good enough."

"But the princess didn't want to?" asked Rosie, hanging on Suvita's every word.

Suvita nodded. "The princess had already met the love of her life," she replied, "and he was not of royal blood. When her father found out, he was very angry, and ordered her never to see her true love again! So one night the princess ran away from the palace."

Rosie gasped. She'd never had to find a runaway princess before – especially one who was all grown-up, as the missing princess would be by now! But whenever Rosie had met a little princess, they'd always needed her help, and it sounded very much as if this runaway princess did too.

"When the maharajah learned that his daughter was gone, he was furious," explained Suvita, "but as he has grown older, he has also grown to regret his anger. He wants to make up with her."

"But she still hasn't come home?" Rosie asked, feeling sad as she listened to the story.

"No, and no one knows where she is," replied Suvita. "The maharajah sent messengers throughout the kingdom to plead for the princess to come home. They posted notices in every town and village. But still she did not return."

"What did the maharajah do next?" asked Rosie.

"He offered a reward to anyone who could tell him where the princess was," Suvita said, pulling a dry sari off the washing-line. Rosie took two corners and, together, the girls began to fold it. "And he offered a reward to anyone who knew where the Ring of the Maharani could be found."

"The Ring of the Maharani?" Rosie echoed. "What's that?"

"It's a diamond ring," explained Suvita. "The diamond is said to be the biggest and most dazzling stone in the whole kingdom!"

"Oh!" Rosie gasped. "It sounds beautiful."

"The ring has been passed down from princess to princess for generations," Suvita went on. "It belonged to the maharani: the maharajah's wife and the princess's mother. When she died, it passed to the princess."

"And the princess was wearing it when she left the palace?" Rosie guessed.

Suvita nodded solemnly. "Neither the princess, nor the ring, has ever been seen again!"

Chapter Four

"That's such a sad story," said Rosie.

Suvita nodded. "Many people think that the princess is dead," she said. "The maharajah fears that he will never see his daughter again. He's very depressed." She pointed at the brown saris on the washing-line. "Yesterday his messengers announced that the maharajah wants us only to wear colours which are as gloomy as his heart."

"So that's why you're dyeing all these beautiful saris brown!" Rosie exclaimed, and Suvita nodded.

Rosie thought for a moment or two. "I think I'll still go to the palace," she said slowly. "Maybe I can help the maharajah."

Suvita smiled at her. "Come into the shop and I'll draw you a map."

Rosie followed her new friend into the small wooden shop. It was quite dark inside, but the shelves were full of rolls of material in dazzling colours.

"Will all these beautiful silks have to be dyed brown too?" Rosie asked in dismay.

"I'm afraid so," Suvita sighed. Then her face brightened. "But I have one sari that will *never* be dyed! Would you like to see it?"

"I'd love to!" Rosie said eagerly.

Suvita hurried away and returned carrying a carved wooden chest. She opened it and took out a silk sari in rich shades of blue and purple, with a beautiful embroidered pattern running along its entire length.

"It was my mother's," Suvita explained. "I never saw her wear it, but I remember her

sitting by the fire, embroidering the pattern."
Tears came into her eyes. "She gave it to me
just before she died."

"It's beautiful," Rosie said.

Suvita smiled proudly. "She gave me this
poem too," she added, putting the sari down
carefully on a nearby table and taking a
yellowed piece of paper from the box.
"Would you like to hear it?"

Rosie nodded.

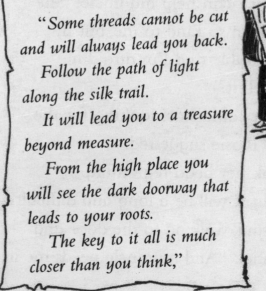

*"Some threads cannot be cut
and will always lead you back.
    Follow the path of light
along the silk trail.
    It will lead you to a treasure
beyond measure.
    From the high place you
will see the dark doorway that
leads to your roots.
    The key to it all is much
closer than you think,"* read Suvita.

"What does it mean?" asked Rosie.

Suvita frowned. "I'm not sure," she replied slowly. "I think my mother meant the Great Silk Trail."

Rosie looked at Suvita blankly "What's that?"

"It's an ancient road that leads from the harbour to all the silk-trading cities in India," explained Suvita. "I'm going to follow the trail when I'm older, and find the treasure in the poem. Then I can help my uncle." She sighed. "He's been so kind to me, but his business is in trouble and I'm afraid he may have to sell it."

"Maybe you could start looking for the treasure now," Rosie suggested.

Suvita shook her head regretfully. "Unfortunately, it will be a long and difficult journey," she said, walking to the door and picking up a stick. "And my uncle needs me in the shop at the moment." She smiled at Rosie. "But luckily for you, the journey to the palace is much easier!" And she began to draw a map with the stick, in the earthen floor.

Rosie watched her for a moment, but her gaze was soon drawn back to the beautiful sari. Suvita glanced up and smiled to see Rosie staring at it.

"Would you fold it up and put it back in the box?" she asked. "My hands are dirty now."

Rosie nodded eagerly. As she carefully picked the sari up, the delicate fabric billowed in the breeze from the door and Rosie got a closer look at the embroidery. She saw a cluster of elephants and, a little further along, a group of peacocks, their tails fully spread. At the end of the silk, there seemed to be a mountain fortress.

As Rosie began to fold the sari, her eye was caught by a single gold thread that sparkled and flashed. It ran right through the sari from end to end, stopping at the fortress. The more Rosie stared at it, the brighter it seemed to shine in the dark room.

Rosie glanced up to tell Suvita, but her eye was caught by the map which her friend was drawing on the floor. Rosie frowned. She looked back at the sari and then at the map again, and she began to tremble with excitement.

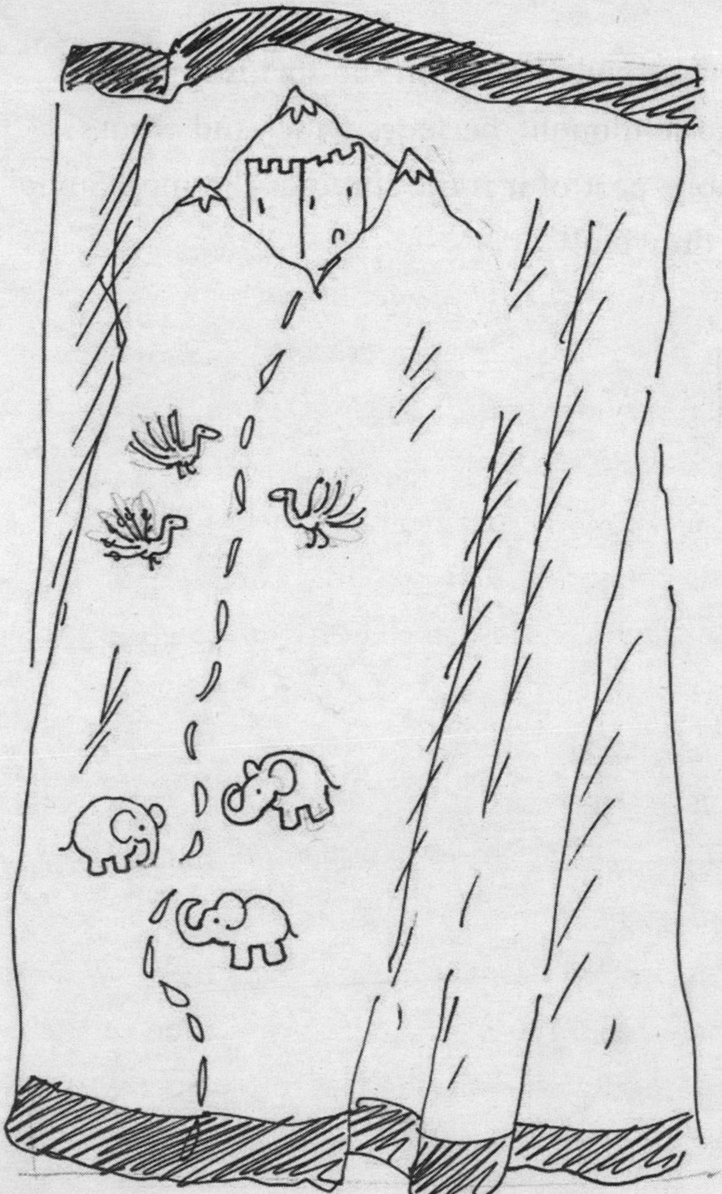

The embroidery on the sari is a map! Rosie thought, her eyes wide. And what's more, part of it is the same as the map Suvita is drawing!

Chapter Five

"Suvita!" Rosie cried. "Look at this!"

She hurried over to her friend and held the embroidered part of the sari out over the map.

Suvita stared at the sari, then at the map she'd drawn. "It's the same!" she whispered in amazement. "I never realized before that the embroidery is a map of our very own kingdom!"

"But your map is smaller," Rosie pointed out. "The sari map covers more ground. Look at this thread." And she pointed out the shining golden thread to Suvita.

Suvita's face lit up. "Now I know what my

mother's poem means!" she cried. "She wasn't talking about the Great Silk Trail, she was talking about the sari. This golden thread must be the path of light!"

"Where does it lead?" Rosie asked eagerly, examining the embroidered fortress.

"That's the Ramanpur Fortress," Suvita explained. "I recognize it now. It was built to guard the northern borders of our kingdom, but our soldiers don't use it any more, and it's just a ruin. It's not that far from here!" She clapped her hands with excitement and beamed at Rosie. "I can travel there and back in one day, and that means I can go and look for the treasure right away! I might even find it before my uncle gets home!"

She rushed out into the yard to the water pump and washed her hands quickly. Then she pulled off the old green sari she was wearing. Underneath she wore a little top

and a long underskirt. Rosie watched, fascinated, as Suvita began expertly wrapping her mother's sari around herself.

"If I'm going on an adventure, I shall need my mother's map!" Suvita laughed, throwing the end of the sari over her shoulder.

"Good idea," Rosie agreed, peering at the embroidered map hanging down her friend's back. "And I'll be able to help you read it, as most of it is behind you!"

Suvita paused. "Does that mean you're coming with me?" she asked, her face breaking into a smile.

Rosie nodded. "I can go to the palace afterwards," she replied. "And perhaps I'll find out something about the missing princess along the way."

"The Ramanpur Fortress is too far to walk," said Suvita as she locked up the shop. "We'll have to hire a horse. And I know just the place." She pointed to the elephants on the sari map. "The watering-hole."

"What's that?" asked Rosie.

"It's where travellers come to buy supplies and hire horses," explained Suvita. "You can hire elephants there too."

"Elephants?" Rosie's eyes lit up. "I love elephants! Will we see any?"

"Of course," Suvita laughed.

After a short walk, the girls reached the

watering-hole. Rosie was thrilled when she saw how many elephants there were. Most of them were standing in a large pool, keeping cool by playfully spraying each other with water from their trunks. Meanwhile, the young boys who were their minders sat chatting in the shade, waiting for work.

As Suvita walked on ahead, Rosie couldn't help overhearing a conversation nearby. A tall bearded man, dressed in black, was talking to a girl in a threadbare pink sari.

"What do *you* want?" the man asked rudely, staring down at the girl. "Haven't I told you to stop bothering me?"

"Please, sir, you haven't paid for the fruit I gave you," the girl explained timidly.

The man sighed loudly, took a few coins from his moneybag and flung them to the ground at the girl's feet. Then he turned and stalked away without another word.

What a horrible man! Rosie thought indignantly. She picked up one of the coins and handed it to the girl, who smiled gratefully at her. Then Rosie hurried after Suvita.

Suvita had stopped and was looking around. "Ah, there he is!" she exclaimed, as Rosie caught up with her. "Anil, over here!"

A bright-eyed boy wearing a white turban came towards them. Rosie was delighted to see that an enormous elephant was following him.

"Rosie, this is my good friend, Anil," said Suvita.

"Hello." Anil beamed at Rosie. "Pleased to meet you."

Before Rosie could reply, the elephant tapped Anil with her trunk.

"Mimi's feeling left out!" laughed Anil, scratching the elephant's chin gently. "Rosie, this is my elephant, Mimi. She wants to say hello to you!"

Thrilled, Rosie held out her hand and Mimi patted it gently with her trunk. The elephant's skin felt warm and wrinkly.

"What are you doing here, Suvita?" asked Anil, as Rosie stroked Mimi's ears.

"We're on a special quest," replied Suvita, "and we need a horse. But I only have a few rupees."

Anil looked thoughtful. "I know someone who has an animal you could hire for very little," he said at last. "I'll go and find him. But I want to hear all about your quest when I get back!" And he dashed off, leaving Rosie and Suvita to play with Mimi.

"Behold, ladies!" Rosie heard Anil shout
from behind her a few moments later.

She and Suvita turned round.

"Here is your noble steed!" Anil declared.
He was hurrying towards them, grinning
widely, and leading a scruffy-looking little
donkey that brayed noisily in greeting.

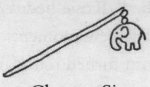

Chapter Six

Rosie and Suvita started to laugh. The donkey was braying so loudly that everyone around them began covering their ears.

Anil stopped and beamed at the girls. "This is Ajay," he announced. "His name means 'invincible'."

"He doesn't look very invincible!" Suvita laughed.

Rosie stroked the donkey's long ears, and Ajay nuzzled her arm softly. "He's very friendly," Rosie said, smiling.

"Now tell me about the quest!" Anil said eagerly.

He listened as Suvita showed him the map

on her sari, and explained that they were going in search of a treasure.

"I wish I could come with you," Anil sighed when Suvita had finished, "but I have to wait here for work. Make sure you are careful on your journey."

"We will, and we'll tell you all about it when we get back," Suvita promised. Then she and Rosie scrambled onto Ajay's back, and the sturdy little donkey set off.

"Goodbye," Rosie and Suvita called, waving at Anil and Mimi.

"Hee-haw!" Ajay added, as if he didn't want to be left out.

They headed along the trail and out into the countryside. Rosie was surprised to see that the trees and fields were lush and green.

"It's beautiful," Rosie sighed. "I expected India to be dry and dusty."

"The countryside is green because the monsoon season has just finished," Suvita explained. "It rains for months. Sometimes I think that the rain will never stop, but it always does."

"Oh, look!" Rosie cried, pointing at a large garden just ahead of them. Through some golden gates she could see fountains and flowers, and even several peacocks! "There are the peacocks from the sari map!"

"That's the maharajah's royal park," Suvita replied.

Ajay trotted past the gates and on through several small villages. Rosie saw people cutting sugar cane in the fields and washing clothes in the river.

"We're making good progress," Rosie remarked as she saw a forest ahead of them. "Ajay might not be a fine stallion, but he's doing a great job."

"Hee-haw!" the little donkey agreed.

Suddenly Rosie and Suvita heard the sound of galloping hooves behind them. As Suvita drew Ajay to the side of the road to let the horse pass, Rosie glanced round. She saw a man dressed all in black swiftly approaching. As he drew nearer, Rosie recognized him as the man who had been so rude to the fruit-seller at the watering-hole.

Instead of riding on past, the man reined in his horse and smiled charmingly at the

girls. "Good day, ladies," he said, gazing
intently at them. "My name is Timir." And
he bowed to them from his saddle.

Suvita smiled back, but Rosie didn't.

"Girls, this is a very dangerous road,"
Timir went on gravely. "Don't you know
that there are bandits in these parts?" He
pointed at the forest. "There's a gang of
thieves who lurk in those trees. They
wouldn't think twice about robbing you

in broad daylight." He shook his head. "You really should have a guide, someone who can look after you. Where exactly are you going?"

Suvita opened her mouth to reply, but Rosie spoke up quickly.

"We're fine on our own, thank you," she said firmly, "and we won't be alone for much longer anyway, because we're meeting someone here."

Suvita was obviously surprised, but she didn't say anything. Rosie tried not to look nervous as Timir's black eyes studied her intently. Then he nodded his head.

"I will bid you farewell then," he snapped, and galloped off.

"What's the matter, Rosie?" asked Suvita. "Why did you tell that nice man that we were meeting someone?"

Quickly Rosie explained what she had seen at the watering-hole. "I don't trust him," she finished, and Suvita nodded.

"He certainly does-n't sound very nice!" she exclaimed.

"We are better off
without him." She shook
the reins and Ajay trotted on.
Gradually, the trail became narrower,
and the countryside more mountainous.
It was starting to get much hotter too. But,
at last, Suvita reined Ajay to a halt.

"Look, there's the fortress, Rosie," she
said, pointing ahead. "We're nearly there!"
Rosie stared at the mountain that
towered in front of them. About halfway

up, on a rocky outcrop, a fortress with turrets had been cut out of the grey stone. It looked like it had been abandoned many years ago, for the rocky walls were crumbling and one of the turrets had collapsed.

"This is the last part of the sari map," said Rosie, staring at the silk hanging over Suvita's shoulder. "The golden thread definitely ends here."

"We're at the end of the path of light!" Suvita said eagerly. She and Rosie slid off Ajay's back, and led him over to a tiny stream which flowed between the rocks. The donkey immediately began to drink.

"What do we do now?" asked Rosie as Suvita tied Ajay's reins to a tree.

"Remember the poem," Suvita replied. "After following the path of light, it said, *From the high place you will see the dark doorway that leads to your roots.*"

"Hmm, *From the high place*," Rosie repeated thoughtfully. "Maybe it means the fortress! Shall we climb up to it and see what we can see from there?" she suggested.

Suvita nodded in agreement and the girls went over to the foot of the mountain. Steps had been carved out of the rock, so they could climb quite easily to the massive wooden doors at the entrance to the fortress.

The doors were old and looked ready to fall apart. They hung ajar and Rosie and Suvita peeped into a huge entrance hall, which had been carved deep into the side of the mountain. A wide and winding wooden staircase swept upwards from the hallway to the top of the fortress, but the stairs were rotten and crumbling.

"We must be careful," Suvita said, as they went over to the staircase. "Some of these stairs have almost fallen to pieces!"

Rosie nodded and cautiously started to climb the stairs. The silent, decaying fortress had an eerie feeling about it. The stairs creaked alarmingly as the girls made their way upwards, and the noise echoed round the hall.

"HEE-HAW!" came a loud bray suddenly.

Rosie jumped. "That's Ajay!" she gasped, wondering what had alarmed the donkey. But at that moment, the step she was standing on cracked and gave way.

"Help!" Rosie screamed as she plummeted

through the hole. At the last minute she managed to grab onto the stair above her and hang on, her legs flailing above the huge drop below.

"Rosie!" Suvita cried anxiously, and rushed to help her friend. But Rosie could feel herself slipping . . .

Chapter Seven

"I can't hold on!" Rosie yelled, struggling to get a grip on the wood as it slipped through her grasp. She lost her grip with one hand and felt sure she was going to fall, but, just in time, Suvita grabbed Rosie's other hand and hauled her upwards.

As Suvita pulled her up, Rosie managed to get a firm hold on the stairs and, eventually, her feet found solid wood again.

Rosie sat on the staircase and grinned shakily at her friend."Thanks, Suvita," she said.

"You're welcome," Suvita replied, keeping hold of Rosie's hand.

The girls continued climbing and it wasn't long before they emerged onto the flat roof of the fortress. It was so high up that the girls had a good view over the surrounding countryside.

Rosie stared out over the land below. There were no fields in this part of the kingdom, and all she could see were trees and bushes. In fact, one tree in particular caught Rosie's eye. It was very big and gnarled and it stood on a hillock below them, right opposite the mountain. Its long, twisted roots grew above the ground and trailed down over the side of the hill.

"I can't see anything that looks like a dark doorway," Suvita remarked.

"Neither can I," said Rosie. She pointed at the gnarled tree. "What sort of tree is that? I've never seen one like it before."

"Oh, that's a banyan tree," Suvita explained. She shaded her eyes and glanced up at the sky, where the sun blazed. "Rosie, we *must* get into the shade now. It's nearly midday."

"OK," Rosie agreed, wiping her face. It was really hot, and she would be glad to get out of the sun for a little while. As Suvita went over to the stairs, Rosie took one last look at the strange banyan tree. The sun was shining through its tangled roots and, quite suddenly, Rosie was reminded of the poem. *From the high place you will see the dark doorway that leads to your roots.*

Rosie stared hard at the roots of the banyan tree. Suddenly, something shifted into focus. Behind two of the largest roots, she thought she could see a dark opening, like a hole in the ground!

"Suvita!" she called excitedly.

Suvita hurried over.

"Look!" Rosie pointed at the tree. "I think

there's an opening between the roots of the banyan tree! Could that be the 'dark doorway' from the poem?"

"Oh!" Suvita gasped, her face lighting up with excitement. "I think you're right, Rosie!"

The girls carefully made their way back down the rickety staircase as quickly as they could. Then they dashed out of the fortress and into the shade of the banyan tree.

Rosie knelt down and pushed aside the roots, which hung like a curtain over the hole they had seen from the fortress. A narrow passage stretched away into darkness.

"Look, Suvita, it's a tunnel!" she cried. "Let's go in!"

Rosie squeezed between the roots, with Suvita close behind. They crawled along on their hands and knees until they emerged into a large underground chamber. Although it was gloomy, the girls were able to see a little because of the bright sunlight that streamed in along the tunnel.

"It's big!" Rosie said, her voice echoing in the empty space.

"But there's nothing here," Suvita pointed out.

"Maybe your mum *hid* the treasure," Rosie suggested. "Let's look around."

The two girls began to search the cavern, but they couldn't find anything at all. They were just about to give up, when Suvita suddenly cried out, "Rosie! I've found a hole in the wall!"

Rosie rushed over to her friend. Underneath an overhanging ledge of rock was a small dark opening.

"Is there anything inside?" Rosie asked breathlessly.

Trembling with excitement, Suvita carefully reached into the hole. "Oh!" she gasped, drawing out a small wooden box with an elaborate gold lock.

"I wonder what's inside!" said Rosie excitedly.

Suvita tried to open the box, but her face fell. "It's locked," she sighed. Then she brightened. "But there's a blacksmith in our village who will be able to open it. Let's take it home with us."

"Let me save you the trouble!" said a menacing voice behind them.

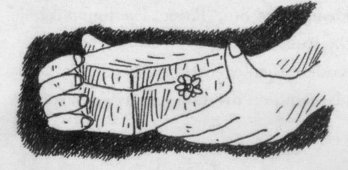

Chapter Eight

Rosie and Suvita spun round. Timir was standing behind them, a smug grin on his face.

"I did warn you, girls," he said, striding forwards and snatching the box from Suvita's hands. "There really *are* bandits about!" And he threw his head back and roared with laughter.

"Give that back!" Suvita demanded furiously.

Timir ignored her, and rattled the box curiously. "What's in it?" he asked.

"I don't know," Suvita snapped. "How did you find the cavern?"

Timir grinned. "I heard you telling that elephant boy you were going to look for treasure," he explained, "so I followed you here. After I passed you on the road, I just hid in the bushes until you overtook me again." He gave an unpleasant laugh. "For someone as clever as me, it was really rather easy!"

Suvita and Rosie looked at each other in dismay. How could they

get the box back from Timir? He was much bigger than they were!

"I tried to follow you into the fortress," Timir went on, "but that stupid donkey of yours made such a noise, I had to stop."

Rosie frowned. So Ajay had tried to

warn them that Timir was coming!

"You've been very clever," she said, stepping forwards. She knew that if she could distract Timir for long enough, she might be able to grab the treasure back. "But do you think you can get the box open?"

"I'm sure I can," Timir boasted. He felt in his pockets. "I have something which might force it—"

At that moment, Rosie darted at him and made a grab for the box. But Timir was too quick for her. He jumped backwards, holding the box teasingly out of Rosie's reach.

"Do you think you can outwit me?" he sneered. "Don't be ridiculous! I'm leaving with the treasure and there's nothing you can do about it!" He strode back towards the tunnel. "I've been very nice to you so far. But if you try to follow me, there'll be trouble!"

Chuckling, he crawled off down the

tunnel. Rosie and Suvita glanced at each other in desperation.

"We're not going to let him get away, are we?" demanded Rosie.

"Of course not!" Suvita cried. "After him!"

The girls dived into the tunnel. When they crawled out from between the roots of the banyan tree, Timir was already mounted on his horse and about to make his escape.

But Rosie and Suvita could hardly believe their eyes: Anil was running towards them!

"What's Anil doing here?" Rosie panted.

Anil jumped bravely into Timir's path and began to shout, waving his hands in the air and clearly trying to stop the bandit.

"Out of my way!" roared Timir. He shook the reins and his horse galloped straight towards Anil, its hooves flying.

"He's going to run Anil down!" Suvita wailed in horror.

Chapter Nine

"Get out of the way, Anil!" Rosie shouted, her heart in her mouth. She could see that Timir wasn't going to stop, and Anil would be badly trampled by the big black horse!

"Stop, Timir!" Suvita screamed, her face pale with fear. But it was clear that the bandit had no intention of reining in his horse.

Suddenly an ear-shattering trumpet call filled the air. It was followed by the sound of heavy footsteps, and the next moment, Mimi the elephant came crashing through the bushes and charged straight towards Timir.

As the girls watched, Mimi stretched out her trunk, wrapped it around the bandit, and lifted him clean off his horse.

The horse reared in surprise, but Anil ran up and grabbed the it's reins.

"Help!" Timir shouted frantically, struggling to free himself from the elephant's trunk. "Let me go!"

But Mimi hung onto him tightly and Timir was helpless.

"Anil!" Suvita exclaimed as she and Rosie ran over to him. "That was so brave! You could have been hurt!"

"I'm fine," Anil said, grinning. "Thanks to Mimi!"

"We're so glad to see you both," Rosie said gratefully. "Mimi did brilliantly, but what are you doing here?"

"After you left, I saw Timir go after you," Anil explained. "Everyone at the watering-hole knows he's usually up to no good, so I decided to follow him."

"Thank goodness you did!" Suvita sighed.

"When I arrived I saw him crawling out from under the tree," Anil went on, "and when I saw that Ajay was here, but you weren't, I got suspicious and tried to stop him."

"You were right," Rosie told him. "Timir *was* up to no good! He stole a little wooden box Suvita found. It's in his pocket."

"Mimi!" Anil called. "Shake! Shake!"

Rosie and Suvita couldn't help laughing as Mimi turned Timir upside down and began to shake him like a salt shaker.

"Stop!" Timir shouted crossly, "I'm getting dizzy!"

At that moment the little wooden box tumbled out of his pocket. Rosie immediately picked it up and handed it to Suvita. Then they petted Mimi, who had now turned Timir the right way up again.

"Thank you for all your help, Anil!" laughed Suvita. "And you too, Mimi. Now we must get this box back to the village, where Raju the blacksmith will be able to open it."

And so they all set off, Anil on Timir's horse, the girls on Ajay the donkey, and Mimi still clutching the grumbling bandit.

Once back at the village, Suvita led the way to the blacksmith's shop.

Raju the blacksmith was in his yard hammering horseshoes out of iron. He was a big, strong man and he wore a leather apron.

"Hello, Suvita," he called, waving at her. "How nice to see you, but who are your friends, and why is that man being held by an elephant?"

"This is Rosie and Ajay the donkey," Suvita said with a smile. "And this is Anil and his elephant, Mimi. But *he's* no friend of mine!" she added, pointing at Timir, who scowled.

Quickly Suvita told Raju the whole story. When she had finished, the blacksmith frowned and turned to Anil. "Bring the bandit this way, please," he said.

Anil and Mimi followed the blacksmith over to a large wooden stake in the middle of the yard. The blacksmith held onto Timir

tightly and Mimi
unwound her trunk.
The blacksmith
then picked up a
rope, wrapped it
round Timir and
tied him securely
to the post.

"You'll pay for
this!" Timir yelled,
red with fury.

But the blacksmith ignored him and
turned to Suvita. "Now, let's go into my
workshop," he suggested. "And I'll try to
open this wooden box."

Rosie, Suvita and Anil followed Raju
inside, leaving Mimi, Ajay and Timir's horse
in the yard, drinking water from a trough.

It was very hot inside because a furnace
blazed in one corner. Suvita handed Raju the

box and the blacksmith examined it closely.

"Hmmm," he said, pointing to the keyhole. "This lock is only a dummy!"

"You mean, it's not the real lock?" asked Rosie, looking puzzled.

The blacksmith nodded. "The box is very cleverly made," he went on, his eyes twinkling. "The real lock is somewhere else . . ." He turned the box over. "Ah! Here it is!"

There, on the bottom of the box, was an indentation in the shape of an elephant.

"This is a block lock," explained Raju. "I'm afraid that we won't be able to open the box without the correct block key."

"But I don't have the key!" Suvita said, her face falling.

Rosie stared at the elephant-shaped indentation. The shape reminded her of something. Suddenly, she turned to look at the hairpin in

Suvita's long black hair — the hairpin which had the tiny elephant hanging from it.

"I think I know where the block key is!" Rosie cried.

"Where?" asked Suvita in surprise.

"Right there," Rosie said, pointing at Suvita's hairpin.

"Oh!" Suvita gasped, putting her hand to her hair and feeling the hairpin. She pulled it out with trembling fingers. "Of course!"

With a smile the blacksmith handed her the box. "It's your box," he said kindly. "So *you* must open it."

Carefully, Suvita slotted the elephant from her hairpin into the indentation on the box. It fitted perfectly and the bottom of the box sprang open.

"How clever!" murmured Suvita. But then she gasped in wonder, for inside the box, on a piece of red silk, sat a gold ring set with a square-cut, sparkling diamond.

Rosie had never seen anything like it. As the light from the furnace caught the jewel, it sent sparkling beams flashing into every corner of the workshop.

"It's beautiful!" murmured Rosie.

"It's more than beautiful," said the black-smith, his face alight with wonder. "It is the Ring of the Maharani!"

Chapter Ten

"Oh!" Rosie exclaimed, her gaze fixed on the exquisite diamond. She remembered the story Suvita had told her about the Ring of the Maharani and how it had vanished along with the missing princess. "Are you sure, Raju?"

The blacksmith nodded. "I've seen pictures of it," he replied. "I have no doubt that this is the Ring of the Maharani!"

Rosie glanced at Suvita. She looked very confused. So did Anil.

"I don't understand," Suvita said in a low voice.

"Well, my dear, if it was your mother who

hid the ring," Raju began, his eyes shining with excitement, "then *she* must have been the missing princess!"

Rosie and Anil gasped. But Suvita didn't say a word; she just stared at the blacksmith in shock.

"And that means *you* are a princess!" the blacksmith went on elatedly. Then, turning on his heel, he dashed out of the workshop and into the street. "Everyone, listen to me!" he yelled. "The maharajah's granddaughter is in my workshop! Suvita, niece of Bansi the silk trader, is the daughter of the missing princess!"

"Rosie, Anil, can this be true?" Suvita asked in amazement.

"If this is the Ring of the Maharani, then I think it must be!" Rosie replied.

"Look," added Anil, pointing at the box. "There's something underneath the silk."

Carefully, Suvita drew back the silk to reveal a piece of paper. Eagerly she took it out and started to read.

"It's from my mother," she said, with tears in her eyes. "It says that she *was* the missing princess, and that she ran away to marry my father."

"But why did she hide the ring?" asked Rosie.

Suvita looked at the letter again. "She says that she hid it so it would be safe until her father was ready to forgive her. But that if I've found the box, then it means that she and my father died before they could be reconciled with the maharajah. My mother wants me

to know that they loved me very much . . ."
Suvita's voice tailed away, and Rosie put an
arm around her friend.

"So what happens now?" Anil whispered.

"My mother writes that I should go to the
palace to see my grandfather," Suvita said in
a rush. "And that I should wear the Ring of
the Maharani on my finger!"

"Ahem!" A cough at the door made
Suvita, Rosie and Anil swing round. A short,
roly-poly man with a very kind face stood
there smiling at them.

"Uncle Bansi!" cried
Suvita, rushing over to
hug him. "You're back!"

"What's going on?"
asked Uncle Bansi, looking
bewildered, but returning
his niece's hug warmly.
"There's a crowd of

people in the blacksmith's yard who seem to think you're a princess!"

"Look, Uncle," said Suvita, and she showed him the box with the ring inside.

Uncle Bansi's eyes almost popped out of his head. "The Ring of the Maharani!" he breathed.

"This explains everything, Uncle," Suvita said, handing him the letter.

Uncle Bansi read it through and his eyes shone with tears. "I always knew there was something special about your mother, Suvita," he murmured. "I wish she and your father had told me their secret. I would have kept it safe." He beamed at his niece. "But, no matter, it seems my little Suvita is actually a little princess!" And he bowed low before her.

"Oh, Uncle Bansi," Suvita laughed, "I'm still the same old Suvita!" She took Rosie's hand. "Rosie, say hello to my uncle. Uncle, I couldn't have found the ring without Rosie and Anil and Mimi."

"And Ajay the donkey!" Rosie reminded her, and there was a loud *hee-haw* from outside which made them all smile.

"I'm very pleased to meet you," Uncle Bansi said warmly to Rosie, and he nodded in greeting to Anil. "And now, my dear," he went on, turning to his niece, "you'd better do exactly what the letter from your beloved mother says, and go straight to the palace. I have a feeling the maharajah will want to see you."

"And remember to put on the ring," added Rosie.

Carefully Suvita took the Ring of the Maharani from the box and slid it onto her finger.

Then Uncle Bansi led them out of the blacksmith's workshop and immediately a deafening cheer went up. The yard was

crammed with people now, all of them eager
to see the ring on Suvita's hand.

"Make way for the princess!" called Raju
the blacksmith, proudly, clearing a path
through the crowd.

Anil turned to Suvita. "Would you and
Rosie like to ride to the palace on Mimi,
Suvita. I mean, Your Royal Highness?" he
asked with a smile.

Suvita laughed and nodded. She held out her hand to Rosie and together they walked over to Mimi, who stood guarding a very sulky Timir. At a word from Anil, Mimi slowly knelt down so that Rosie and Suvita could climb onto her back.

Anil jumped on too, sitting cross-legged in front of the girls, to guide the elephant. Rosie, who was behind Suvita, clung onto her friend's waist as Mimi got to her feet again. It was strange to be so high above the crowd, swaying from side to side as the elephant plodded towards the yard gates.

They set off along the street. Behind them came Uncle Bansi on his mule, followed by Raju riding Timir's horse and leading the bandit by the rope that bound his hands. Ajay trotted along next to the horse, braying loudly. Everyone else followed too – nobody wanted to be left out.

As the little procession made its way towards the palace, people came out of their houses to see what all the noise was about. When they heard that the maharajah's granddaughter had been found, they joined the procession, chattering excitedly.

They turned a corner and suddenly a majestic palace came into view. It was a huge building made out of dazzling white marble. It had an enormous dome and a tall, slender tower at each of its four corners.

The crowd gathered at the gates, where soldiers barred their way.

"Suvita, tell them who you are," Rosie said to her friend.

Suvita raised her hand and waved at the captain to get his attention, but before she could say anything, the captain gasped in awe.

"The Ring of the Maharani!" he exclaimed. "Open the gates and let her through!"

Immediately the soldiers rushed to open the heavy golden gates. Mimi tramped inside, followed by Uncle Bansi, Raju and the whole procession.

As they marched towards the palace doors,
an upper window flew open. A man dressed
in a red turban and rich robes of red and
gold burst out onto the balcony, looking
very angry indeed.

"What's all this noise about?" he
demanded furiously.

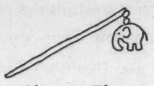

Chapter Eleven

"It's the maharajah!" Suvita whispered to Rosie.

Rosie tried not to look dismayed. The maharajah didn't seem very friendly. What would he do when he heard Suvita's story?

But just then, the maharajah noticed Suvita sitting on the elephant. Rosie saw all the colour drain from his face. He stared at Suvita as if he'd seen a ghost. Then his gaze dropped to her hand, where it rested on Mimi's ear, the Ring of the Maharani sparkling in the sunlight.

"Wait there!" the maharajah cried, and he dashed back inside the palace.

"We'd better get down from Mimi," Suvita said nervously. "I shall have to explain who I am."

Anil urged Mimi to kneel and Suvita and Rosie clambered off the elephant. By the time the maharajah hurried out of the palace doors, followed by his courtiers, Suvita was waiting for him. Rosie felt very nervous indeed as she watched the maharajah approach. Would he believe Suvita's story?

"Your Highness, my name is Suvita, and I am your granddaughter," Suvita began breathlessly. She held her mother's letter out to the maharajah.

"My mother wrote this letter. It explains everything," she went on.

But the maharajah held out his arms. "I need no explanations!" he cried, beaming at Suvita. "I can see my beloved daughter right here in your own face! My dear granddaughter, I can't tell you how happy it makes me that you've come home." And he hugged Suvita, his face alight with happiness and wonder.

At last the maharajah released the little princess. "Your mother, my precious daughter," he asked Suvita gently. "Is she . . . dead?"

Suvita nodded sadly and explained that her mother had died some years ago. The maharajah was saddened by this news, but eventually he wiped the tears from his eyes and turned to the crowd. "Please, welcome my granddaughter, Princess Suvita, home!"

he cried in a loud voice. "My heart has been returned this day."

As Suvita smiled and hugged her grandfather, everyone erupted into cheers of joy, and Rosie and Anil grinned from ear to ear.

"Grandfather, this is my friend Rosie," announced Suvita. "I would never have found out the truth about my mother if it wasn't for her. She was the one who found the map on the sari."

"What map?" the maharajah asked, looking puzzled. "You must tell me the whole story, my dear. But first, let me welcome your friend." He smiled warmly at Rosie. "Rosie is our honoured guest," he announced and Rosie blushed with delight. "And now the

whole kingdom will celebrate!" He clapped his hands. "Send word to the palace kitchens. And summon my musicians and entertainers. We shall all feast together in the gardens!"

As the servants rushed to do the maharajah's bidding, he turned to Suvita and Rosie.

"And now I want to hear all about your adventure," he said eagerly.

The whole crowd fell silent and listened in wonder as Suvita, with Rosie's help, told the story of how she had found the Ring of the Maharani by following the map embroidered on her mother's sari.

"So many people have helped me, grandfather," Suvita said earnestly. "My Uncle Bansi has loved and cared for me ever since my parents died. Rosie was with me every step of the way on my journey to find my mother's ring. Anil and Mimi the elephant saved us from the bandit, Timir, and Raju the blacksmith worked out the secret of how to open the box."

The maharajah raised his hand. "Then I must reward all your friends," he said firmly. He pointed at Anil who was standing next to Mimi. "You, Anil, will be head keeper of the royal elephants, and gallant Mimi will be the lead elephant!"

Anil beamed.

"Timir," the maharajah went on sternly, looking at the sullen bandit, "will spend the next year mucking out the elephants' stables!"

The crowd roared with laughter and Timir glared.

"Ajay the donkey will live in the palace stables, and Raju will become the royal blacksmith," the maharajah continued. "And Bansi, my granddaughter's beloved uncle, will become my ambassador for trade."

Suvita rushed over to hug her uncle, who looked delighted.

"And, Rosie . . ." The maharajah said, turning to her. "What can I give you for returning my granddaughter to me?"

"Nothing," Rosie replied, shaking her head. "I'm just glad that I found the little princess!"

The maharajah smiled at her and clapped his hands. "Then let the celebrations begin!" he announced.

The musicians struck up a lively tune as everyone moved towards the tables, piled with food, that had been set out in the palace grounds. When everyone had eaten their fill, they danced on the lawns and watched the jugglers and acrobats

jump and tumble among the flowerbeds.
Rosie had a wonderful time dancing with
Anil and Suvita, but as people began to leave
the party, she knew that it was time she went
home.

"Suvita, I must go," she whispered, drawing
her friend aside. Anil had already left to take
Mimi to her new living quarters in the royal
stables. "I'll visit again soon, though."

"I'll miss you," Suvita said, smiling at Rosie.
"You were right the whole time, you know!"

Rosie was puzzled. "What do you mean?"

"You asked me if I was a little princess in
disguise," Suvita laughed, "and I really was!"

Rosie laughed too. "I told you so!" she
teased, giving her friend a big hug.
"Goodbye, Suvita."

Immediately a scented breeze swept Rosie
off her feet and, a few moments later, she
found herself back in the castle sewing room

with the picture frame in her hand.

"I'm sure you'll be a fantastic princess, Suvita!" Rosie said happily.

At that moment she heard the sound of running footsteps in the corridor and Luke burst in.

"I just remembered that you and Mum made your party costume from stuff in here, Rosie," he said breathlessly. "What's that in your hand?"

Rosie showed him the picture frame.

"It's great!" Luke said enviously. "I like the picture in the corner. I hope my frame will look that good."

"Oh, it will," Rosie assured him with a grin. "It'll be good enough for a little princess – or maybe a little prince!" she added, laughing.

THE END

Did you enjoy reading about Rosie's
adventure with the Silk Princess?
If you did, you'll love the next
Little Princesses
book!

Turn over to read the first chapter of
The Cloud Princess.

Chapter One

"Thanks for the lift, Mrs Edwards," Rosie Campbell said, getting out of the car. "Bye, Emily."

"Bye, Rosie," Emily said from the back seat.

"Goodbye, love," Emily's mum called. "And remember to take off those muddy wellies before you go indoors!"

Rosie nodded as Mrs Edwards drove away. Rosie's boots were absolutely caked with mud from her school trip to an archaeological dig. The whole class had watched the archaeologists use special tools to scrape away mud from trenches as they hunted for buried Roman artefacts. At the end of the day, everyone in Rosie's class had been allowed to have a go themselves, and Rosie had found a small orange tile! She'd been given special permission to bring it home to show her parents, before it went back to school tomorrow to be displayed with the other finds from the dig.

Rosie tramped up to the front door, carefully stepped out of her boots and went into the grand, echoing hallway. She hung up her coat, then went through to the big, warm kitchen, where her mum and her five-year-old brother, Luke, were sitting at the table.

"Wall. W-A-L-L," Luke was saying as she walked in.

"Well done," Mrs Campbell said. She looked up at Rosie. "Hello, Rosie. Did you have a good day?"

"It was great," Rosie said. She held up her

tile. "I found this on the dig. My teacher said
that it could be a tile from a real Roman
mosaic!"

Mrs Campbell came over for a closer look.
Rosie handed her the little tile.

"I wonder where it came from?" said Mrs
Campbell, turning it over in her hand. "It's

amazing to think that it might have been part of a Roman mosaic made over a thousand years ago, isn't it?"

Rosie nodded eagerly.

"What's a mosaic, Mum?" Luke asked, coming over to see the tile.

"It's a picture or pattern that's made up of thousands of tiny little tiles," Mrs Campbell explained. "The Romans used to have them on their floors and walls."

"Tile. T–I–L–E," Luke said proudly. He grinned at Rosie. "I've got a spelling test tomorrow," he explained. "And I've just *got* to beat Anna this time. She's this girl in my class and she always comes top at spelling. I can't keep getting beaten by a yucky girl!"

Rosie laughed. "Girls aren't yucky, Luke," she said.

Mrs Campbell passed Rosie's tile back to her. "You should have a look at the mosaic upstairs," she said. "It's on the wall of the northern passageway."

Rosie nodded. She'd seen the mosaic before but hadn't paid much attention to it. It was in a particularly draughty stone passageway, so she tended to rush past it as quickly as she could. "I'll go and look at it right now," she said enthusiastically, and headed off in the direction of the stairs.

Rosie was now in the northernmost side of the castle, which got the least sun. She shivered and pulled her school cardigan more tightly around herself as she ran along the passage. This is why I never come along here, she thought. It's freezing!

Rosie turned a corner and spotted the mosaic on the wall a little way ahead. As she drew level with it, she stopped and gazed at it in fascination. It was enormous, longer than Rosie's arms spread out wide, and almost as high as she was. If you stood right up close to the mosaic, all you could see were the thousands of tiny individual ceramic tiles that made up the picture. But as you edged back, and looked at the mosaic as a whole, the picture took shape before your eyes.

The mosaic was edged with a twisty geometric border in red and brown. In the background of the picture itself stood a palatial villa that looked just like the Roman palace Rosie had been studying at school. It had white walls, a terracotta tiled roof, and five marble columns in the centre of the building.

In front of the palace, an old man lay stretched out on a couch. Leaning over him, looking anxious, was a young girl in a white toga with a golden circlet around her head. Rosie felt her heart start to beat more quickly. She was sure that the girl was a little princess!

"Hello," Rosie said to the girl, making a neat curtsey.

All at once, a breeze streamed out of the mosaic, enveloping Rosie in the scent of lavender and the sweet taste of honey. The breeze became a whirlwind, and lifted Rosie right off her feet. Another adventure was beginning . . .

The whirlwind slowed, and Rosie felt her feet touch the ground again. She looked around curiously. She was in a formal garden, with neatly trimmed rectangular lawns, edged with flowering lavender bushes. There was a white marble building in front of her, with stone columns at the entrance. Inside the building, Rosie could see a girl kneeling before a stone altar, with a large basket of fruits and bread by her side. Rosie guessed that the building must be a temple.

The girl was dressed in a white toga, edged with a purple stripe. She had light-brown hair, coiled up neatly in a knot on top of her head, and she carried a satchel on one shoulder.

Rosie hastily looked down at herself

and saw that her school uniform had disappeared. She was now wearing a white toga, with a red sash over one shoulder. The sash was pinned to the white material with a sparkly brooch of red stones set in gold. Around her arms were golden circlets that shone in the sun. Rosie reached up to touch her own hair and found that it was coiled up neatly on top of her head.

I'm in ancient Rome, Rosie thought, feeling tingly with excitement.

Read the rest of *The Cloud Princess* to follow Rosie's adventures!

Little Princesses
The Sea Princess

Katie Chase

Rosie knows a very special secret.
Hidden in her great-aunt's mysterious
Scottish castle are lots of little princesses
for her to find. And each one will
whisk her away to another part of the
world on a magical adventure!

Marissa, the Sea Princess, needs Rosie's help
to find her crown and the Pearl of Wisdom
that will restore order to the underwater kingdom
of Aquatica. However, to find it, the girls must
swim down to the bottom of the ocean and
enter the cave of the Sea Hag.

Join Rosie and meet her exciting new friends,
as she discovers all the Little Princesses.

978 0 099 48842 2